CW00864075
My name is
I am ______ years old
I love my **Tumbi** Book
TUMBI

First Published June 2008

Book Design
Design Difference, Kochi

Printed in India
Standard Press Pvt. Ltd., Sivakasi

Publisher
D C Books
21/3 Shrungar Complex, M G Road, Bangalore, Karnataka, India
D C Kizhakemuri Edam, Good Shepherd Street, Kottayam 686 001, Kerala, India
Website: www.tumbi.org
Email: editorial@tumbi.org

ISBN 978-81-264-1912-8

D C Books: The first Indian Book Publishing House to get ISO Certification

FOLKTALES

THE KING OF BIRDS

RETOLD BY **TANYA MUNSHI**
ILLUSTRATED BY **SREELAL A G**

One evening grandma and all the children were gathered around a fire. The little ones were eagerly waiting for a story from their grandmother.

"Grandma," asked a little child, "If the king of animals is Bhubesi the Lion, then who is the king of birds?"

"That's a very good question," replied grandma. Sensing a story coming up, the children drew closer to her. She said, "You are right, the Lion is the king of animals, but for the birds..... I will tell you a story about the time the birds decided to choose a king."

Right after God finished creating the world and the animals, plants and birds, the great Eagle called a meeting amongst all the birds. Everyone attended the meeting including the Owl, the Bustard and the Warbler.

"As you all know," began the magnificent Eagle, "the Lion Bhubesi is the king of animals. But no one really talks about us. Hence it is my decision that we choose a king amongst us great winged creatures." The moment he spoke, a commotion of birdie chatter rose from the crowd. The Eagle continued in a firm voice, "Since I am the most regal and magnificent bird present, I declare myself to be king."

A soft murmur swept across the crowd. Just then another voice rose bringing the commotion to a silence. "Yes Eagle, you are indeed very majestic. But it is I who should be king, as I have the largest eyes," It was the Owl who spoke. "And since I can see everything that happens, I am wise. A king needs wisdom, more than being regal," said the Owl.

Just then another voice was heard. It was the Bustard who spoke, "While I accept the Eagle's regal bearing and the Owl's wisdom, I declare myself to be king." The Bustard went up to the centre and continued, "Since I am the largest of all the winged creatures, I deserve to be king, as strength is vital for leadership." Again a commotion arose among the birds. While some supported the Eagle, the others supported the Owl and the rest the Bustard.

Just then, a tiny voice intervened, "Excuse me!" It was the Warbler. He was the tiniest of the lot and hence went easily unnoticed. He said, "It is I who should be king."

Everyone burst out laughing. The mere thought of having a tiny bird as their king was very amusing.

"How can you be our king?" The Eagle asked.

"Well, even I should be given an equal chance as everyone else," said the little Warbler. This impressed the assembly of birds and the Eagle spoke, "Well then, we shall have a competition to see who is fit to be king."

They decided to meet in the open grassland the next day. As soon as the sun's rays touched the tip of the tallest mountain, the birds would soar into the sky. The one who flew the highest and touched the hand of God would be declared king.

The birds were awake all night as they eagerly waited for the sun to rise. Just as the sun's rays touched the highest peak, all the birds instantly rose into the air.

But the Warbler had a plan. He knew he was too tiny to fly so high, so he quietly hid under the Eagle's wings. The Eagle was so busy competing that he did not feel the presence of the Warbler.

The birds flew higher and higher. The smaller birds couldn't cope with the heat of the sun and so after a short time they drifted back to earth.

Only the Eagle, the Owl and the Bustard were left. After a while, the Owl was exhausted and he gave up.

Finally, though they were terribly tired, only the Eagle and the Bustard continued flying. But gradually the Bustard was losing out. He told the Eagle, "I can go no further; you are the winner."

On hearing this, the Eagle sounded his victory cry, but just then, the Warbler shot out of the Eagle's feathers. "Not so fast Eagle; you have not won yet," said the Warbler and he flew to touch the hand of God.

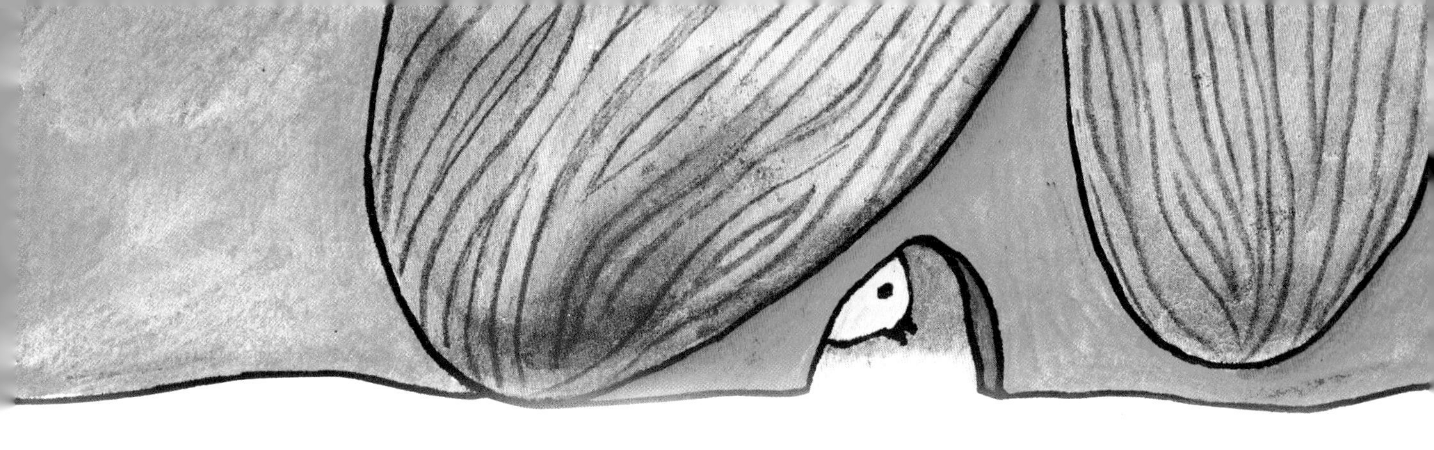

In spite of his efforts, the Eagle could not muster any more strength and glided back to earth. All the birds had seen what had happened and were very angry. When the Warbler reached earth, he did not receive a welcome fit for a king. Instead, all the birds charged at him to pluck his feathers. The Warbler quickly escaped and hid inside a snake hole.

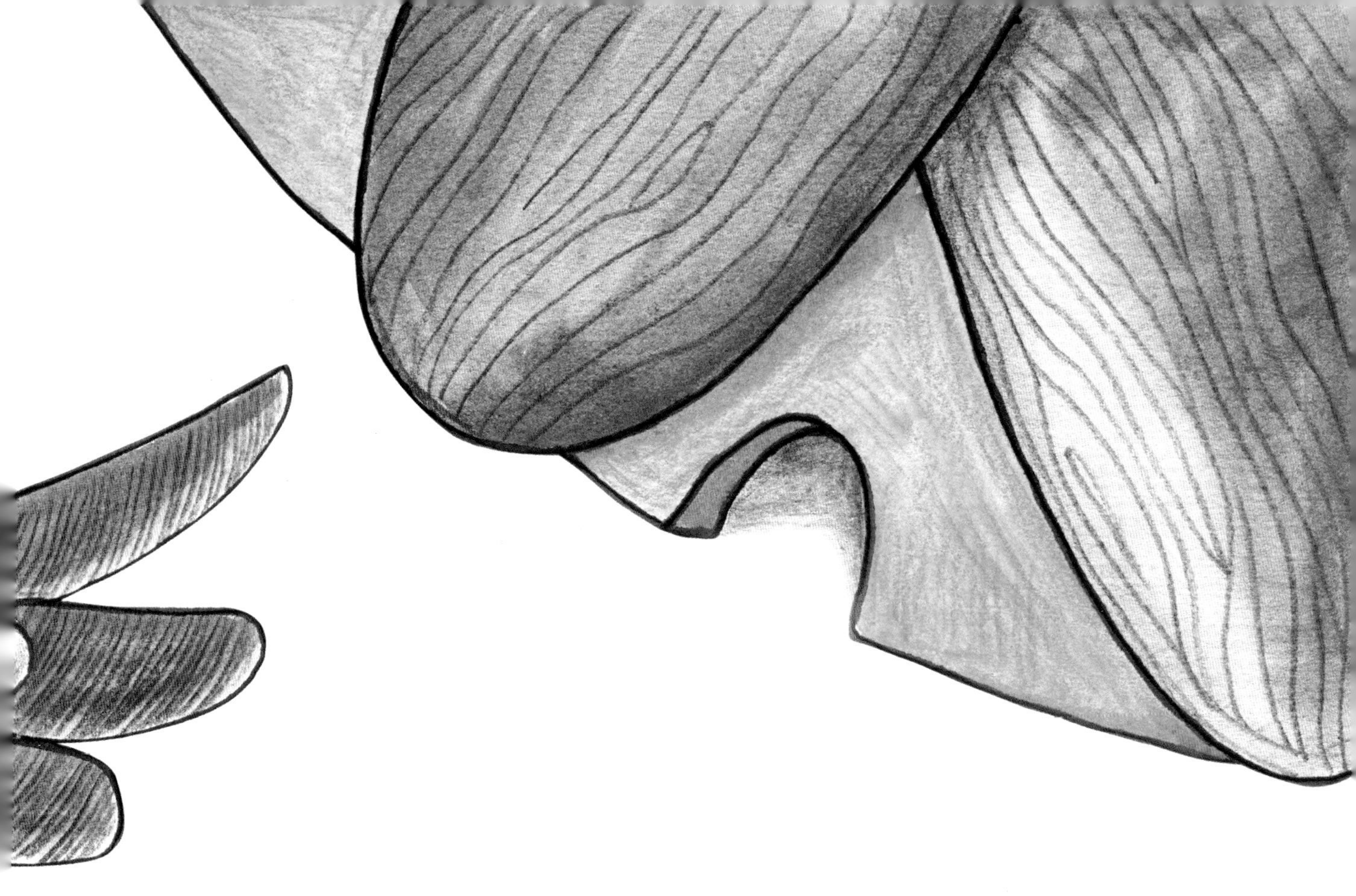

"Come out Warbler," yelled the Bustard, "come and get your reward."

The birds waited all night hoping that the Warbler might come out for food or water. But the little bird did not appear.

At dawn, the Eagle said, "I am tired and hungry. We need not wait together to guard the hole. We can take turns till the Warbler comes out." Since everyone was tired, they agreed to the plan.

"I am not too tired or hungry," said the Owl, "I'll take the first watch; just ensure that someone relieves me in an hour or two."

He waited and waited and it seemed like forever. The Owl was getting weary and decided to watch the hole with one eye open. He closed his right eye and watched the hole with his left eye. After a while, the Owl closed his left eye and kept his right eye open. This went on for quite a while till he forgot to open both his eyes and he fell asleep.

This was what the Warbler had been waiting for; he ran out of the hole and disappeared into the jungle. The Eagle, who was on his way to relieve the Owl, saw the Warbler escape and seeing the Owl asleep cried out, "Wake up, sleepy head. Because of you the Warbler has escaped!"

The Owl was so embarrassed that, to this day he sleeps during the day and hunts by night. As for the Warbler, he keeps fluttering in the forest and hiding all the time and hence never gets caught.

"So grandma," asked a child, "who became the king of birds?"

Grandma smiled and said, "That my child is still undecided as the birds still squabble over who will be king."